Curry Gardens
Ankh-Morpork

Curry with:
Vegetable - 8p
Meat - 10p
Named Meat - 15p
Sweat, and sore Balls of
Pig - 10p
Sweat, and sore Balls of
Fish - 10p
Porn Cracker - 5p

First published in Great Britain in 2019 by Gollancz
an imprint of The Orion Publishing Group Ltd
Carmelite House, 50 Victoria Embankment, London EC4Y 0DZ

An Hachette UK Company

1 3 5 7 9 10 8 6 4 2

A CIP catalogue record for this book is available
from the British Library.

ISBN (Hardback) 978 1 473 22429 2

Typeset by Amanda Cummings
Printed in China

www.gollancz.co.uk

This book belongs to:

DEATH
(AND FRIENDS)
A
DISCWORLD
JOURNAL

Everyone, it is said, has a book inside them. In this library, everyone was inside a book.

. . . Book on book, shelf on shelf . . . and in every one, at the page of the ever-moving now, a scribble of handwriting following the narrative of every life . . .

Terry Pratchett, *Hogfather*

Even anthropomorphic personifications need a place to call their own. In Death's Domain his library provides sanctuary for the Reaper Man to reflect on life, the universe and fine Klatchian curries.

It also contains the life story of every being that has ever existed on the Discworld. People who have already died, obviously, fill their book from cover to cover, and those who haven't been born yet have to put up with blank pages. Those in between . . . well . . . that's up to you.

The first *Discworld Journal* features selected wisdom from Sir Terry Pratchett's most endearing and enduring horseman of the 'Apocralypse'. Aided and abetted by his constant companions, Death will guide you through this journal as you jot down your daily musing, pen your immortal prose or, perhaps more aptly, write your very own life story.

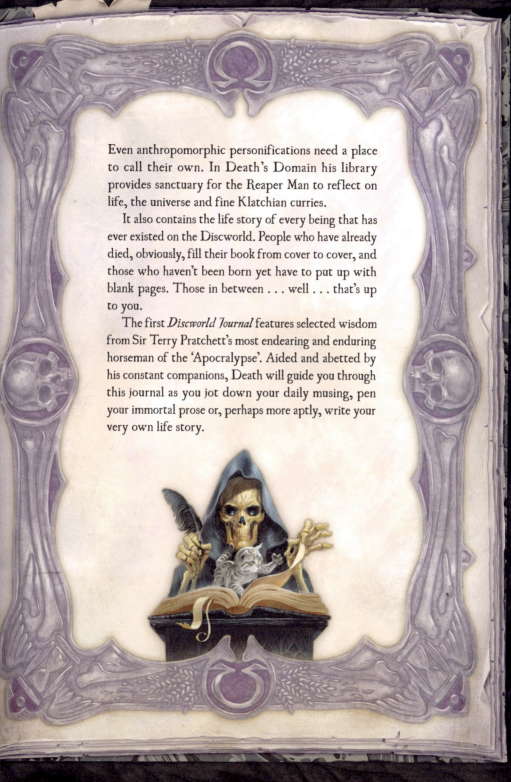

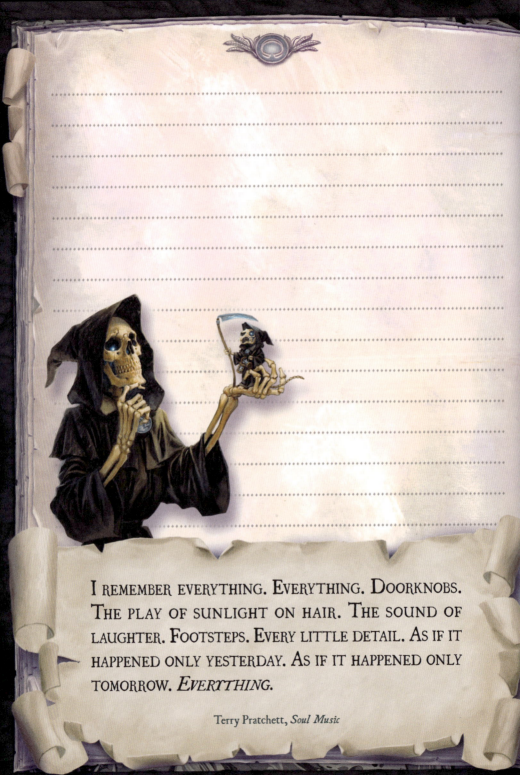

I REMEMBER EVERYTHING. EVERYTHING. DOORKNOBS. THE PLAY OF SUNLIGHT ON HAIR. THE SOUND OF LAUGHTER. FOOTSTEPS. EVERY LITTLE DETAIL. AS IF IT HAPPENED ONLY YESTERDAY. AS IF IT HAPPENED ONLY TOMORROW. EVERYTHING.

Terry Pratchett, *Soul Music*

. . . In the house of Death there is no time but the present. (There was, of course, a present *before* the present now, but that was also the present. It was just an older one.)

Terry Pratchett, *Reaper Man*

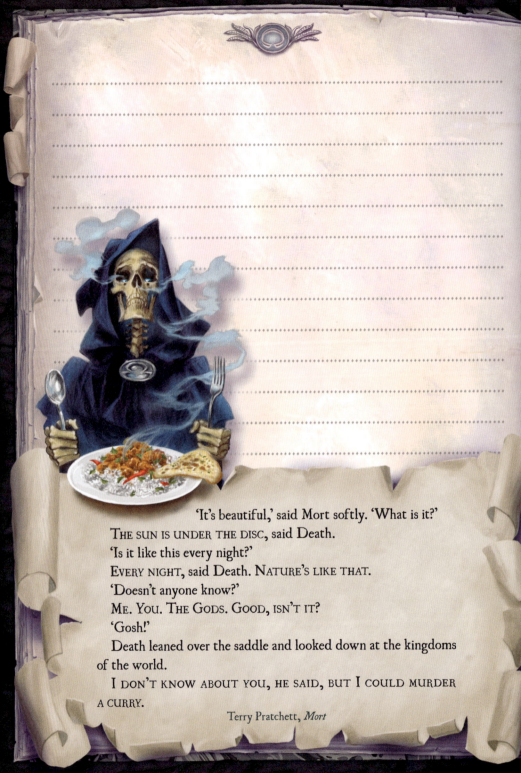

'It's beautiful,' said Mort softly. 'What is it?'

THE SUN IS UNDER THE DISC, said Death.

'Is it like this every night?'

EVERY NIGHT, said Death. NATURE'S LIKE THAT.

'Doesn't anyone know?'

ME. YOU. THE GODS. GOOD, ISN'T IT?

'Gosh!'

Death leaned over the saddle and looked down at the kingdoms of the world.

I DON'T KNOW ABOUT YOU, HE SAID, BUT I COULD MURDER A CURRY.

Terry Pratchett, *Mort*

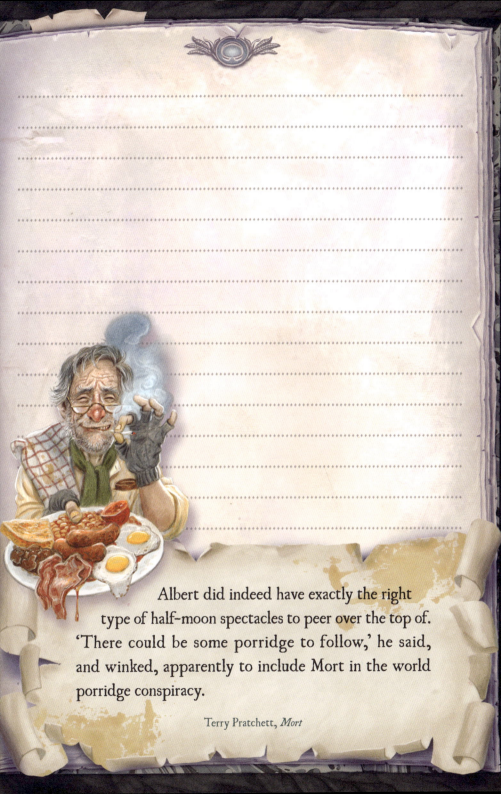

Albert did indeed have exactly the right type of half-moon spectacles to peer over the top of. 'There could be some porridge to follow,' he said, and winked, apparently to include Mort in the world porridge conspiracy.

Terry Pratchett, *Mort*

....
....
....
....
....
....
....
....
....
....
....
....

'All *right*, all *right*.' The raven ruffled its feathers. 'This thing here is the Death of Rats. Note the scythe and cowl, yes? Death of Rats. Very big in the rat world.'

The Death of Rats bowed.

Terry Pratchett, *Soul Music*

In the warm, horsey gloom of the stable, Death's pale horse looked up from its oats and gave a little whinny of greeting. The horse's name was Binky. He was a real horse. Death had tried fiery steeds and skeletal horses in the past, and found them impractical, especially the fiery ones, which tended to set light to their own bedding and stand in the middle of it looking embarrassed.

Terry Pratchett, *Reaper Man*

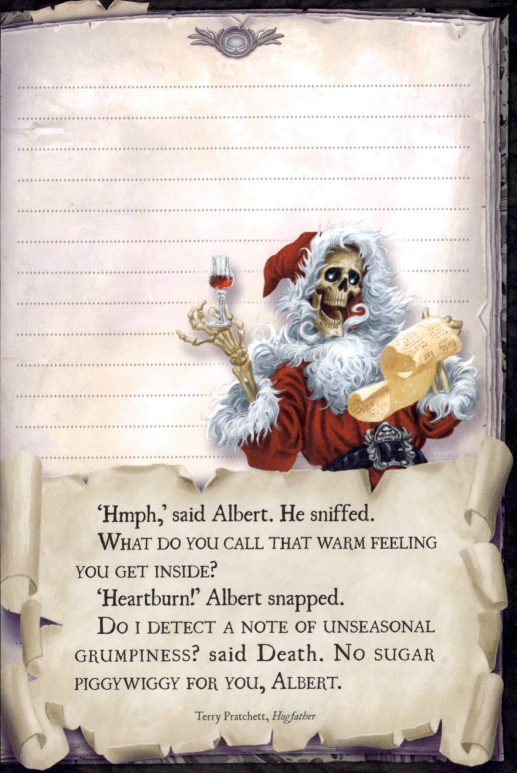

'Hmph,' said Albert. He sniffed.

WHAT DO YOU CALL THAT WARM FEELING YOU GET INSIDE?

'Heartburn!' Albert snapped.

DO I DETECT A NOTE OF UNSEASONAL GRUMPINESS? said Death. NO SUGAR PIGGYWIGGY FOR YOU, ALBERT.

Terry Pratchett, *Hogfather*

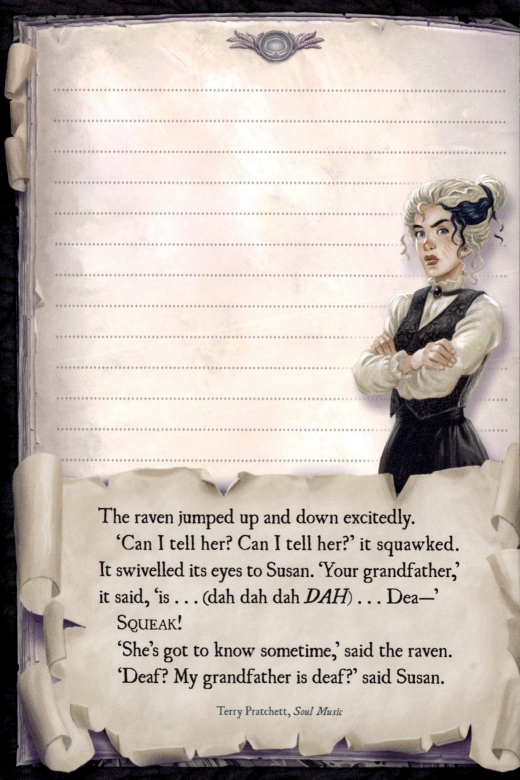

The raven jumped up and down excitedly.

'Can I tell her? Can I tell her?' it squawked. It swivelled its eyes to Susan. 'Your grandfather,' it said, 'is . . . (dah dah dah *DAH*) . . . Dea—'

SQUEAK!

'She's got to know sometime,' said the raven.

'Deaf? My grandfather is deaf?' said Susan.

Terry Pratchett, *Soul Music*

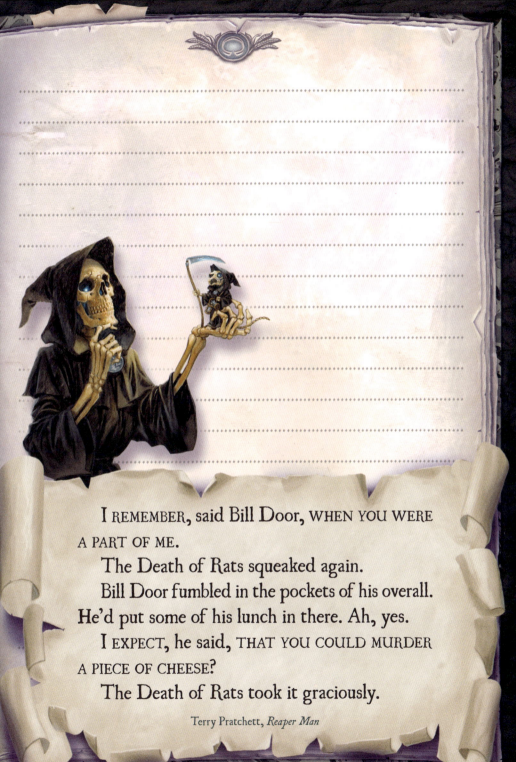

I REMEMBER, said Bill Door, WHEN YOU WERE A PART OF ME.

The Death of Rats squeaked again.

Bill Door fumbled in the pockets of his overall. He'd put some of his lunch in there. Ah, yes.

I EXPECT, he said, THAT YOU COULD MURDER A PIECE OF CHEESE?

The Death of Rats took it graciously.

Terry Pratchett, *Reaper Man*

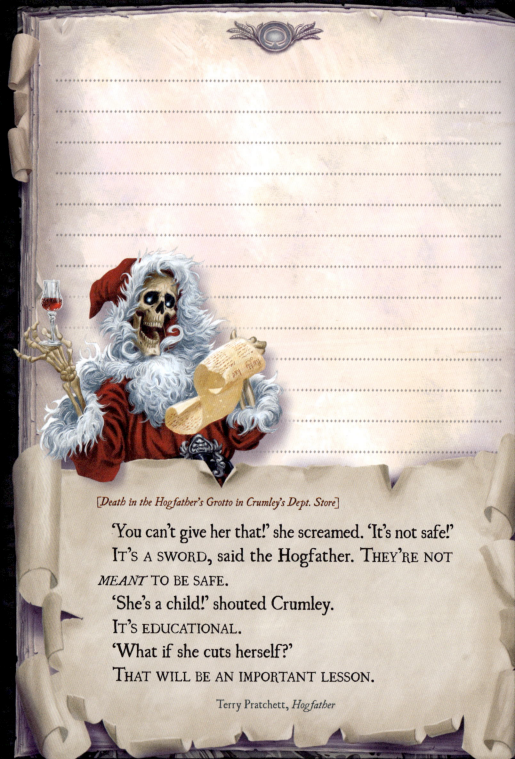

[Death in the Hogfather's Grotto in Crumley's Dept. Store]

'You can't give her that!' she screamed. 'It's not safe!'

IT'S A SWORD, said the Hogfather. THEY'RE NOT *MEANT* TO BE SAFE.

'She's a child!' shouted Crumley.

IT'S EDUCATIONAL.

'What if she cuts herself?'

THAT WILL BE AN IMPORTANT LESSON.

Terry Pratchett, *Hogfather*

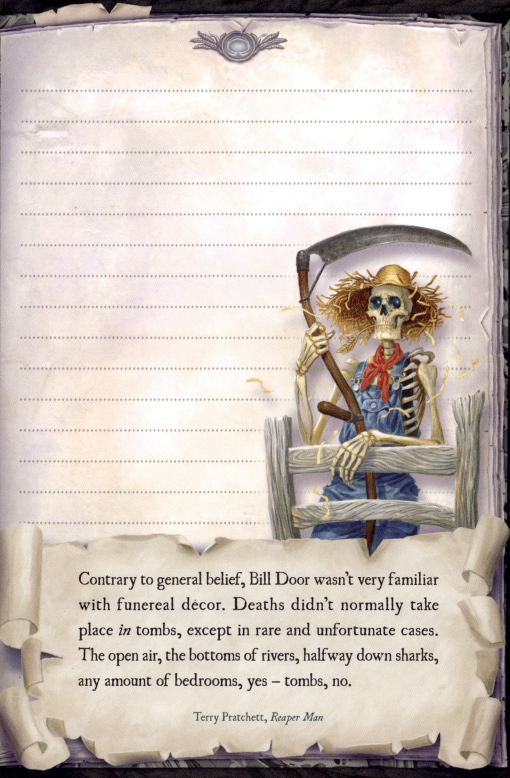

Contrary to general belief, Bill Door wasn't very familiar with funereal décor. Deaths didn't normally take place *in* tombs, except in rare and unfortunate cases. The open air, the bottoms of rivers, halfway down sharks, any amount of bedrooms, yes – tombs, no.

Terry Pratchett, *Reaper Man*

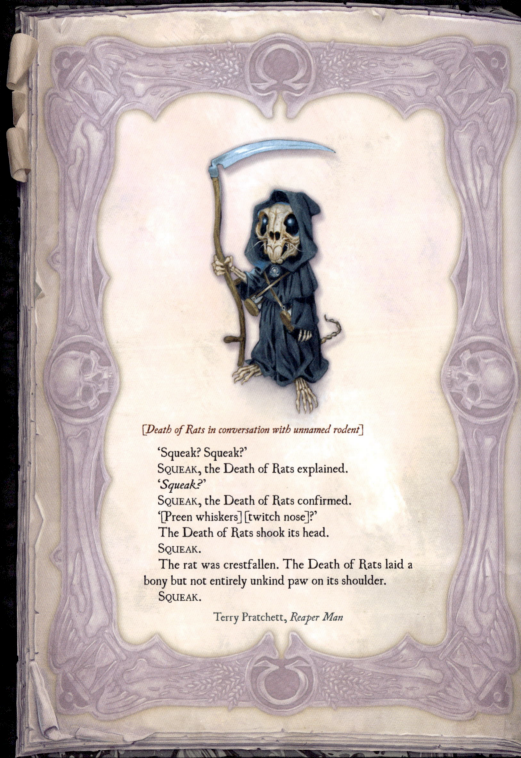

[Death of Rats in conversation with unnamed rodent]

'Squeak? Squeak?'
SQUEAK, the Death of Rats explained.
'Squeak?'
SQUEAK, the Death of Rats confirmed.
'[Preen whiskers] [twitch nose]?'
The Death of Rats shook its head.
SQUEAK.
The rat was crestfallen. The Death of Rats laid a bony but not entirely unkind paw on its shoulder.
SQUEAK.

Terry Pratchett, *Reaper Man*

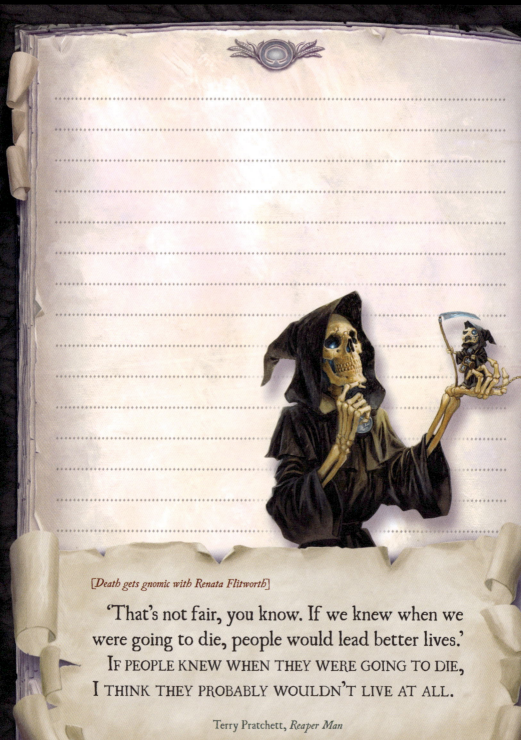

'That's not fair, you know. If we knew when we were going to die, people would lead better lives.'
IF PEOPLE KNEW WHEN THEY WERE GOING TO DIE, I THINK THEY PROBABLY WOULDN'T LIVE AT ALL.

Terry Pratchett, *Reaper Man*

[Death and Albert discuss the nature of change]

YOU FEAR TO DIE?
'It's not that I don't want . . . I mean,
I've always . . . it's just that life is a habit
that's hard to break . . .'

Terry Pratchett, *Reaper Man*

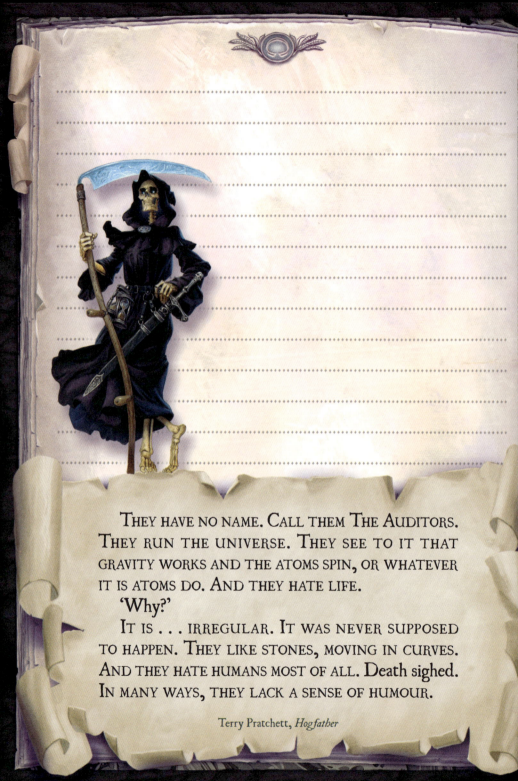

They have no name. Call them The Auditors. They run the universe. They see to it that gravity works and the atoms spin, or whatever it is atoms do. And they hate life.

'Why?'

It is . . . irregular. It was never supposed to happen. They like stones, moving in curves. And they hate humans most of all. Death sighed. In many ways, they lack a sense of humour.

Terry Pratchett, *Hogfather*

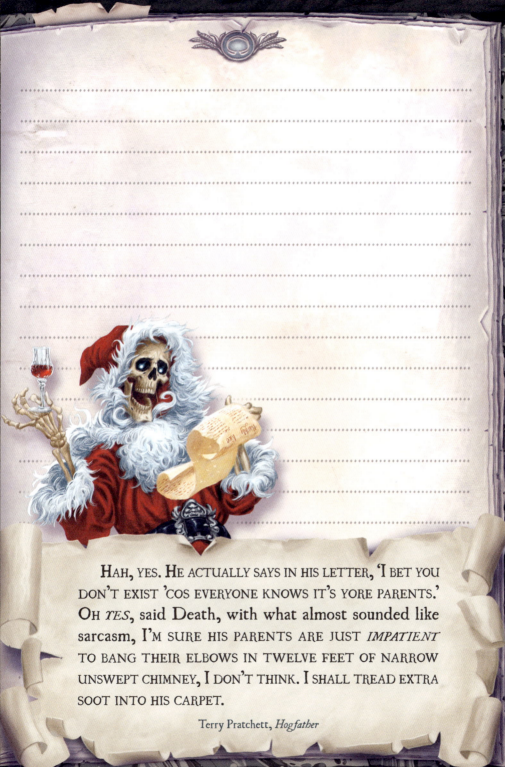

HAH, YES. HE ACTUALLY SAYS IN HIS LETTER, 'I BET YOU DON'T EXIST 'COS EVERYONE KNOWS IT'S YORE PARENTS.' OH *YES*, said Death, with what almost sounded like sarcasm, I'M SURE HIS PARENTS ARE JUST *IMPATIENT* TO BANG THEIR ELBOWS IN TWELVE FEET OF NARROW UNSWEPT CHIMNEY, I DON'T THINK. I SHALL TREAD EXTRA SOOT INTO HIS CARPET.

Terry Pratchett, *Hogfather*

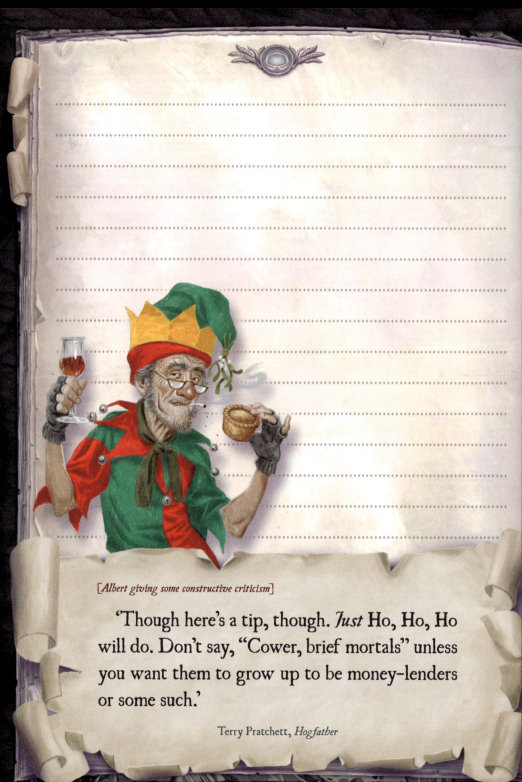

[*Albert giving some constructive criticism*]

'Though here's a tip, though. *Just* Ho, Ho, Ho will do. Don't say, "Cower, brief mortals" unless you want them to grow up to be money-lenders or some such.'

Terry Pratchett, *Hogfather*

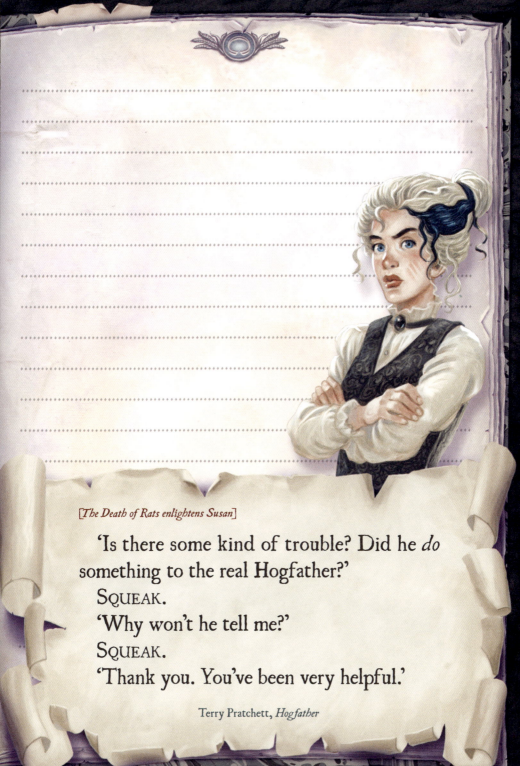

'Is there some kind of trouble? Did he *do* something to the real Hogfather?'

SQUEAK.

'Why won't he tell me?'

SQUEAK.

'Thank you. You've been very helpful.'

Terry Pratchett, *Hogfather*

'This is a battlefield, isn't it,' said the raven patiently. 'You've got to have ravens afterward.' Its freewheeling eyes swivelled in its head. 'Carrion regardless, as you might say.'

Terry Pratchett, *Soul Music*

YOU NEED TO BELIEVE IN
THINGS THAT AREN'T TRUE.
HOW ELSE CAN THEY *BECOME*?

Terry Pratchett, *Hogfather*

Belief creates other things. It created Death. Not death, which is merely a technical term for a state caused by prolonged absence of life, but Death, the personality. He evolved, as it were, along with life. As soon as a living thing was even dimly aware of the concept of suddenly becoming a non-living thing, there was Death. He was Death long before humans ever considered him; they only added the shape and all the scythe and robe business to a personality that was already millions of years old.

Terry Pratchett, *Reaper Man*

I'VE NEVER BEEN VERY SURE ABOUT WHAT IS RIGHT, said Bill Door. I AM NOT SURE THERE IS SUCH A THING AS RIGHT. OR WRONG. JUST PLACES TO STAND.

Terry Pratchett, *Reaper Man*

THERE'S NO JUSTICE, said Mort. JUST US.

Terry Pratchett, *Mort*

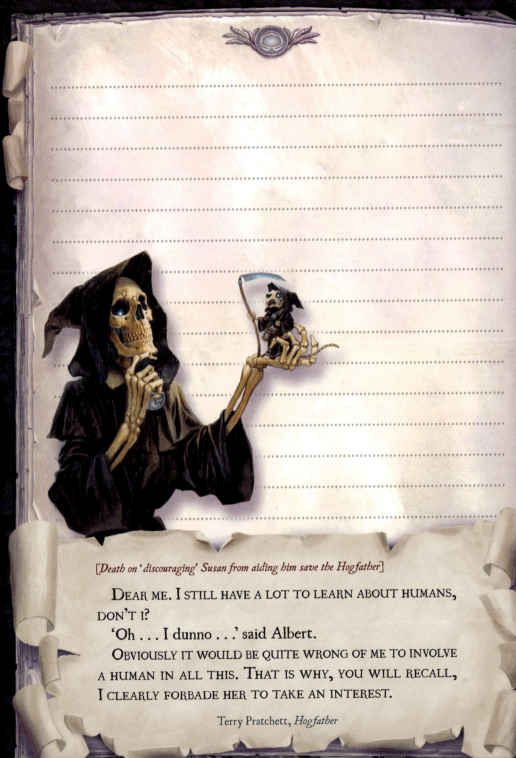

[Death on 'discouraging' Susan from aiding him save the Hogfather]

DEAR ME. I STILL HAVE A LOT TO LEARN ABOUT HUMANS, DON'T I?

'Oh . . . I dunno . . .' said Albert.

OBVIOUSLY IT WOULD BE QUITE WRONG OF ME TO INVOLVE A HUMAN IN ALL THIS. THAT IS WHY, YOU WILL RECALL, I CLEARLY FORBADE HER TO TAKE AN INTEREST.

Terry Pratchett, *Hogfather*

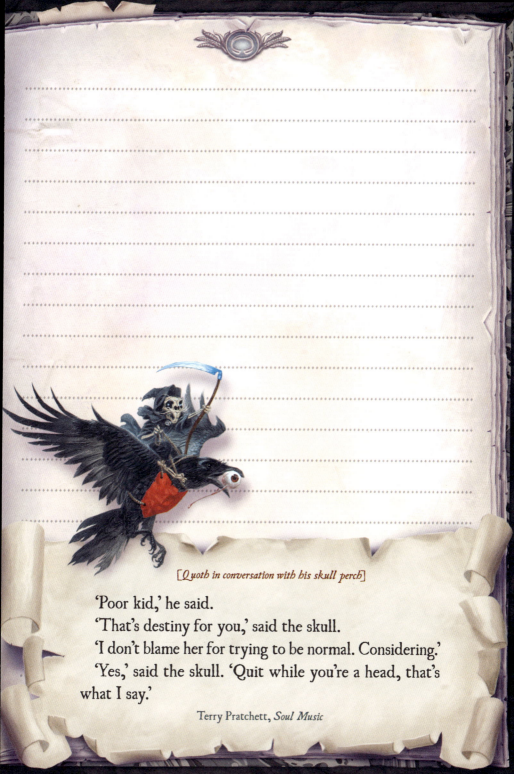

'Poor kid,' he said.

'That's destiny for you,' said the skull.

'I don't blame her for trying to be normal. Considering.'

'Yes,' said the skull. 'Quit while you're a head, that's what I say.'

Terry Pratchett, *Soul Music*

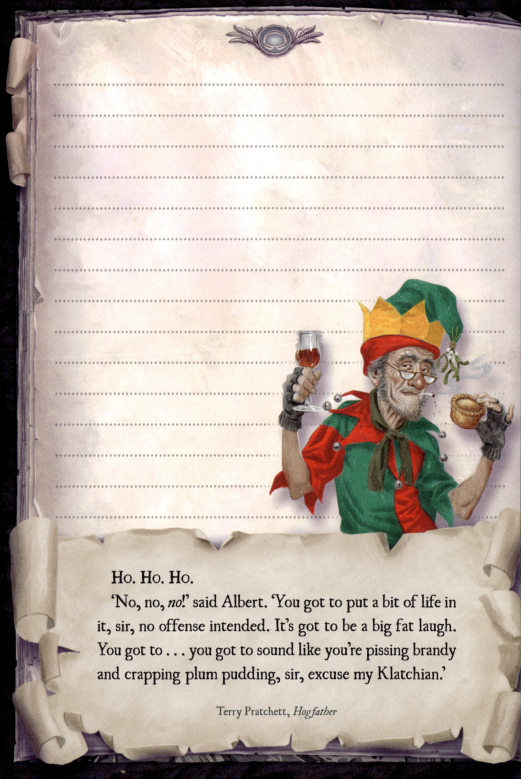

Ho. Ho. Ho.

'No, no, *no!*' said Albert. 'You got to put a bit of life in it, sir, no offense intended. It's got to be a big fat laugh. You got to . . . you got to sound like you're pissing brandy and crapping plum pudding, sir, excuse my Klatchian.'

Terry Pratchett, *Hogfather*

Not a muscle moved
on Death's face, because he hadn't
got any.

Terry Pratchett, *Reaper Man*

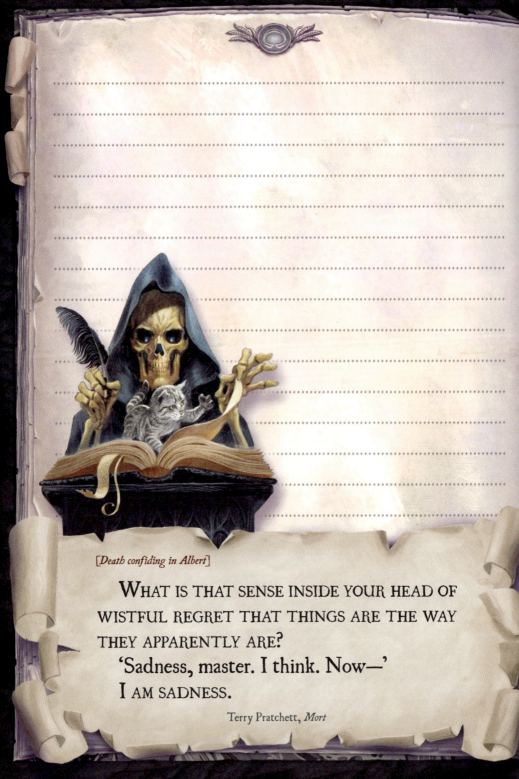

WHAT IS THAT SENSE INSIDE YOUR HEAD OF
WISTFUL REGRET THAT THINGS ARE THE WAY
THEY APPARENTLY ARE?

'Sadness, master. I think. Now—'
I AM SADNESS.

Terry Pratchett, *Mort*

WE HAVE THREE-QUARTERS OF AN HOUR.

'How can you be sure?'

BECAUSE OF DRAMA, MISS FLITWORTH. THE KIND OF DEATH WHO POSES AGAINST THE SKYLINE AND GETS LIT UP BY LIGHTNING FLASHES, said Bill Door, disapprovingly, DOESN'T TURN UP AT FIVE-AND-TWENTY PAST ELEVEN IF HE CAN POSSIBLY TURN UP AT MIDNIGHT.

Terry Pratchett, *Reaper Man*

[*Death in discussion with the spirit of Ipslore the Red, residing in a staff*]

YOU'RE ONLY PUTTING OFF THE INEVITABLE, he said.

That's what being alive is all about.

Terry Pratchett, *Sourcery*

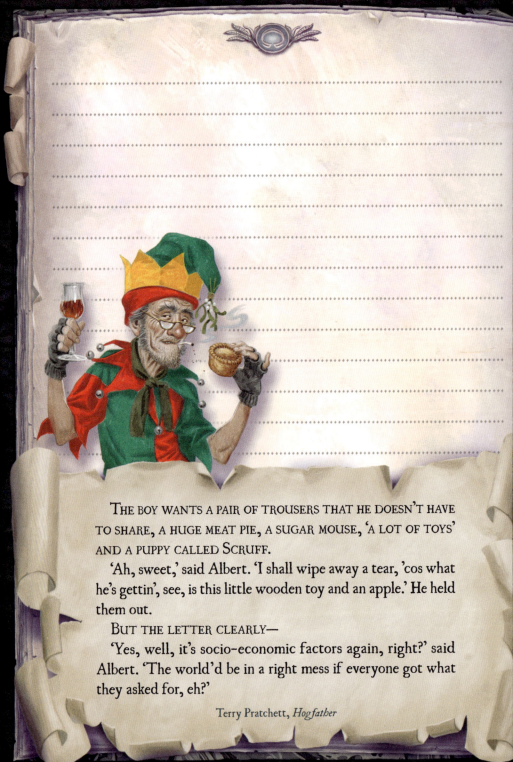

THE BOY WANTS A PAIR OF TROUSERS THAT HE DOESN'T HAVE
TO SHARE, A HUGE MEAT PIE, A SUGAR MOUSE, 'A LOT OF TOYS'
AND A PUPPY CALLED SCRUFF.

'Ah, sweet,' said Albert. 'I shall wipe away a tear, 'cos what
he's gettin', see, is this little wooden toy and an apple.' He held
them out.

BUT THE LETTER CLEARLY—

'Yes, well, it's socio-economic factors again, right?' said
Albert. 'The world'd be in a right mess if everyone got what
they asked for, eh?'

Terry Pratchett, *Hogfather*

S<small>QUEAK</small>!

'Look, you have to lead up to things with humans,' said the raven wearily. One eye focused on Susan again. 'He's not one for subtleties, him. Rats don't argue questions of a philosophical nature when they're dead . . .'

Terry Pratchett, *Soul Music*

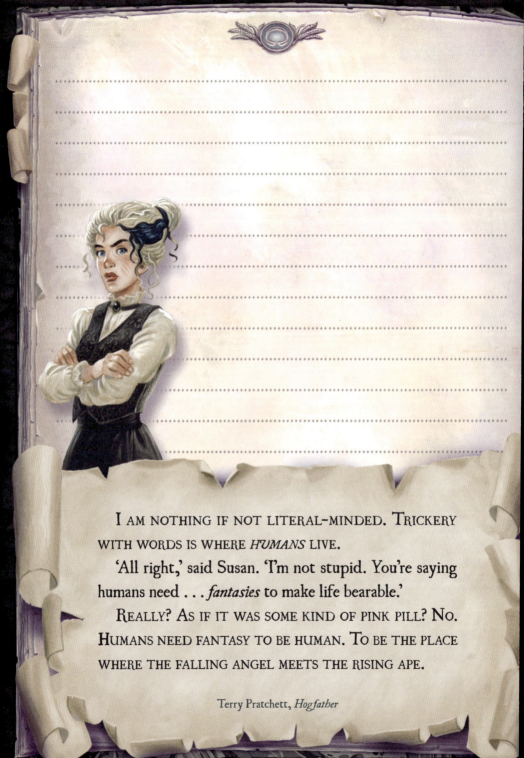

I AM NOTHING IF NOT LITERAL-MINDED. TRICKERY
WITH WORDS IS WHERE *HUMANS* LIVE.

'All right,' said Susan. 'I'm not stupid. You're saying
humans need . . . *fantasies* to make life bearable.'

REALLY? AS IF IT WAS SOME KIND OF PINK PILL? NO.
HUMANS NEED FANTASY TO BE HUMAN. TO BE THE PLACE
WHERE THE FALLING ANGEL MEETS THE RISING APE.

Terry Pratchett, *Hogfather*

'The Pyramids of Tsort by moonlight!'
breathed Ysabell, 'How romantic!'
MORTARED WITH THE BLOOD OF
THOUSANDS OF SLAVES, observed Mort.

Terry Pratchett, *Mort*

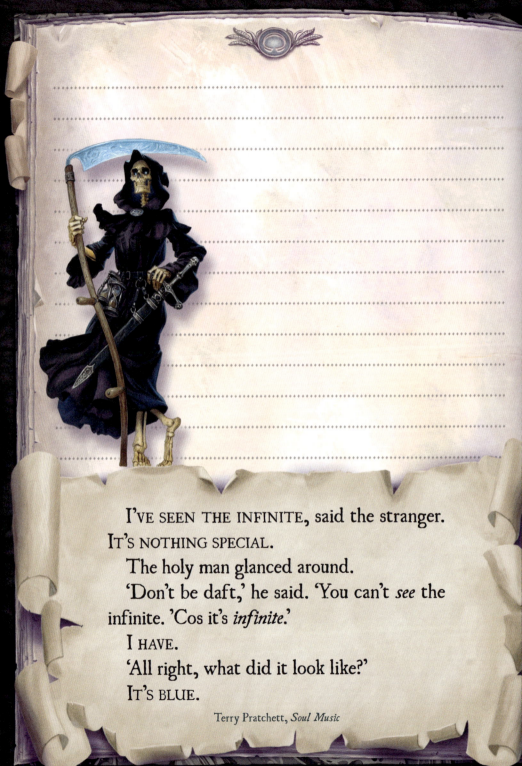

I've seen the infinite, said the stranger. It's nothing special.

The holy man glanced around.

'Don't be daft,' he said. 'You can't *see* the infinite. 'Cos it's *infinite*.'

I have.

'All right, what did it look like?'

It's blue.

Terry Pratchett, *Soul Music*

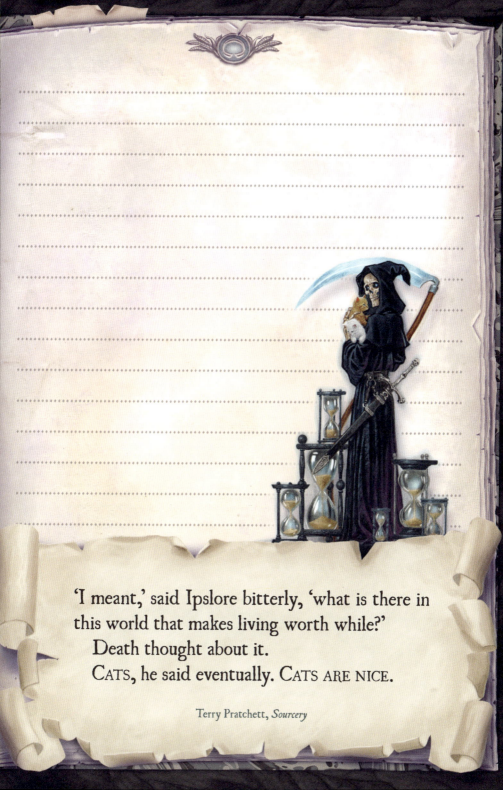

'I meant,' said Ipslore bitterly, 'what is there in this world that makes living worth while?'

Death thought about it.

CATS, he said eventually. CATS ARE NICE.

Terry Pratchett, *Sourcery*

NOW *THAT'S* MUSIC WITH ROCKS IN.

Terry Pratchett, *Soul Music*

Death coughed. I SUPPOSE . . . ?

'Sorry?'

I KNOW IT'S RIDICULOUS, REALLY . . .

'What is?'

I SUPPOSE . . . YOU HAVEN'T GOT A KISS FOR YOUR OLD GRANDDAD?

Susan stared at him.

The blue glow in Death's eyes gradually faded, and as the light died it sucked at her gaze so that it was dragged into the eye sockets and the darkness beyond . . .

. . . which went on and on, for ever. There was no word for it. Even *eternity* was a human idea. Giving it a name gave it a length; admittedly, a very long one. But this darkness was what was left when eternity had given up. It was where Death lived. Alone.

She reached up and pulled his head down and kissed the top of his skull. It was smooth and ivory white, like a billiard ball.

Terry Pratchett, *Soul Music*

Death coughed. I SUPPOSE . . . ?

'Sorry?'

I KNOW IT'S RIDICULOUS, REALLY . . .

'What is?'

I SUPPOSE . . . YOU HAVEN'T GOT A KISS FOR YOUR OLD GRANDDAD?

Susan stared at him.

The blue glow in Death's eyes gradually faded, and as the light died it sucked at her gaze so that it was dragged into the eye sockets and the darkness beyond . . .

. . . which went on and on, for ever. There was no word for it. Even *eternity* was a human idea. Giving it a name gave it a length; admittedly, a very long one. But this darkness was what was left when eternity had given up. It was where Death lived. Alone.

She reached up and pulled his head down and kissed the top of his skull. It was smooth and ivory white, like a billiard ball.

Terry Pratchett, *Soul Music*

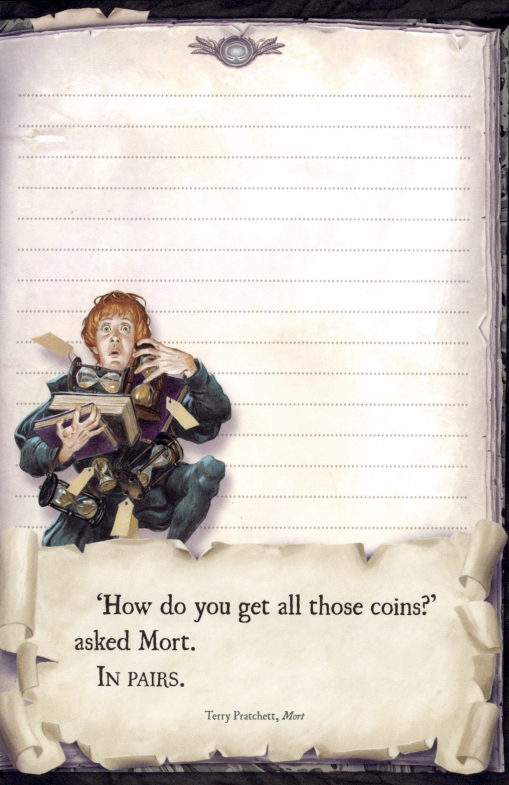

'How do you get all those coins?'
asked Mort.

IN PAIRS.

Terry Pratchett, *Mort*

Rincewind had been told that death was just like going into another room. The difference is, when you shout, 'Where's my clean socks?', no one answers.

Terry Pratchett, *Eric*

He looked up as Mort came in, keeping one calcareous finger marking his place, and grinned. There wasn't much of an alternative.

Terry Pratchett, *Mort*

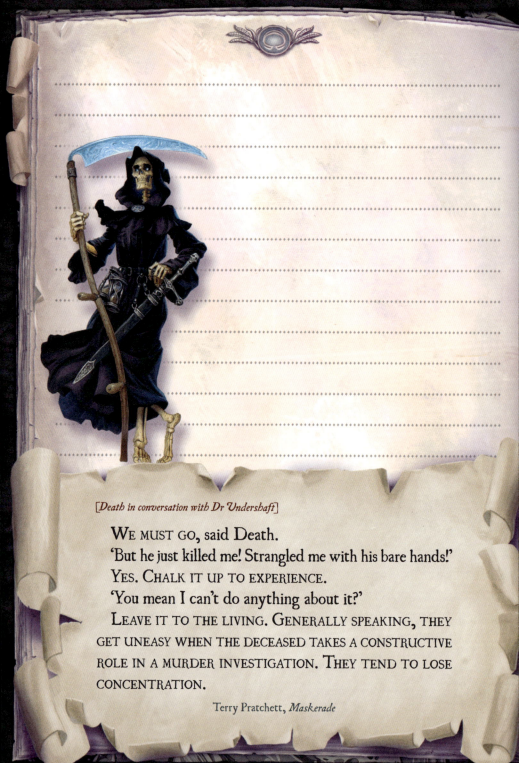

WE MUST GO, said Death.

'But he just killed me! Strangled me with his bare hands!'

YES. CHALK IT UP TO EXPERIENCE.

'You mean I can't do anything about it?'

LEAVE IT TO THE LIVING. GENERALLY SPEAKING, THEY GET UNEASY WHEN THE DECEASED TAKES A CONSTRUCTIVE ROLE IN A MURDER INVESTIGATION. THEY TEND TO LOSE CONCENTRATION.

Terry Pratchett, *Maskerade*

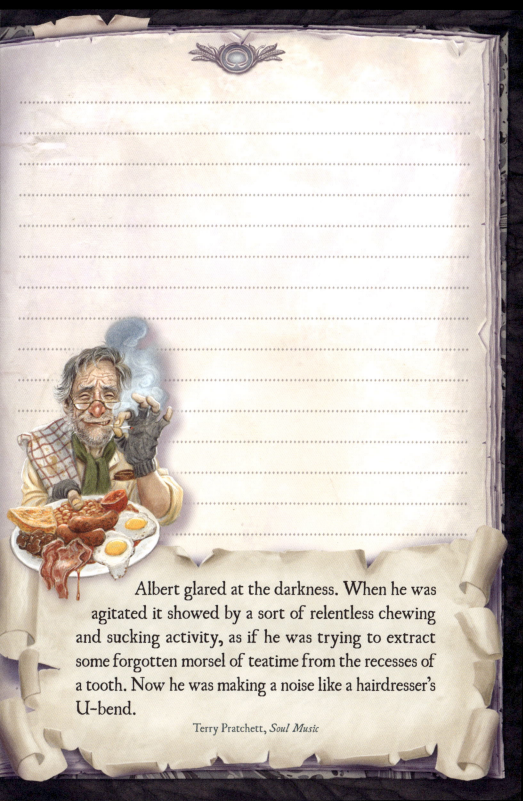

Albert glared at the darkness. When he was agitated it showed by a sort of relentless chewing and sucking activity, as if he was trying to extract some forgotten morsel of teatime from the recesses of a tooth. Now he was making a noise like a hairdresser's U-bend.

Terry Pratchett, *Soul Music*

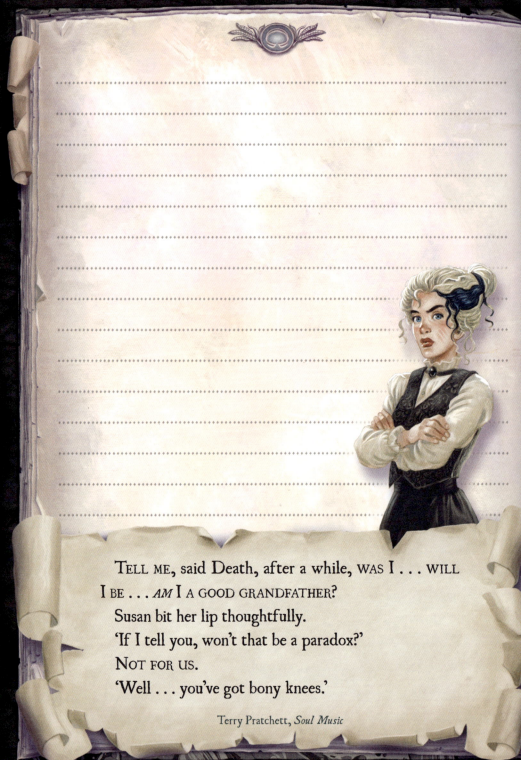

TELL ME, said Death, after a while, WAS I ... WILL I BE ... AM I A GOOD GRANDFATHER?

Susan bit her lip thoughtfully.

'If I tell you, won't that be a paradox?'

NOT FOR US.

'Well ... you've got bony knees.'

Terry Pratchett, *Soul Music*

'And what would humans be without love?'
RARE, said Death.

Terry Pratchett, *Sourcery*

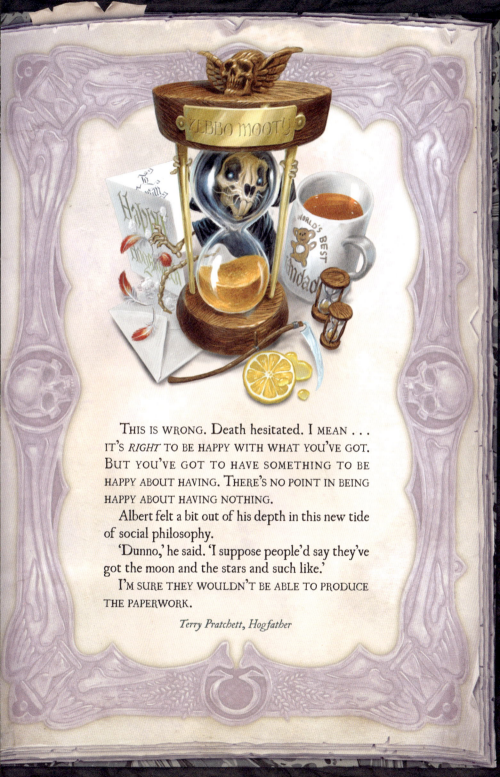

THIS IS WRONG. Death hesitated. I MEAN . . .
IT'S *RIGHT* TO BE HAPPY WITH WHAT YOU'VE GOT.
BUT YOU'VE GOT TO HAVE SOMETHING TO BE
HAPPY ABOUT HAVING. THERE'S NO POINT IN BEING
HAPPY ABOUT HAVING NOTHING.

Albert felt a bit out of his depth in this new tide
of social philosophy.

'Dunno,' he said. 'I suppose people'd say they've
got the moon and the stars and such like.'

I'M SURE THEY WOULDN'T BE ABLE TO PRODUCE
THE PAPERWORK.

Terry Pratchett, Hogfather

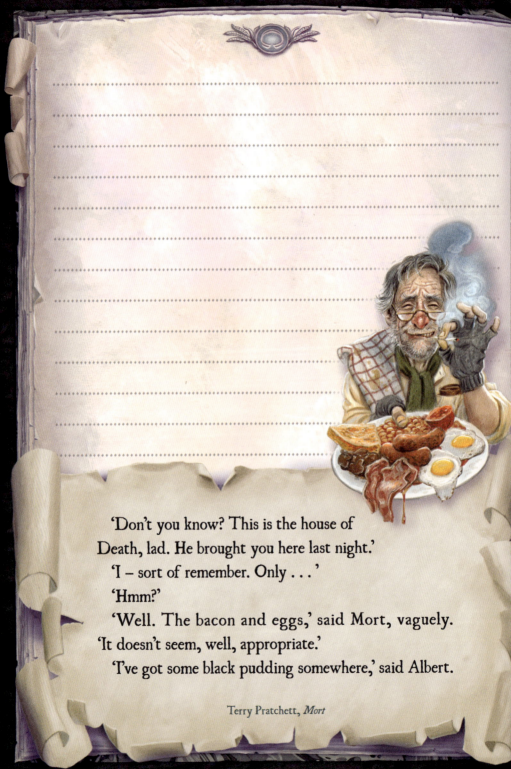

'Don't you know? This is the house of
Death, lad. He brought you here last night.'

'I – sort of remember. Only . . .'

'Hmm?'

'Well. The bacon and eggs,' said Mort, vaguely.
'It doesn't seem, well, appropriate.'

'I've got some black pudding somewhere,' said Albert.

Terry Pratchett, *Mort*

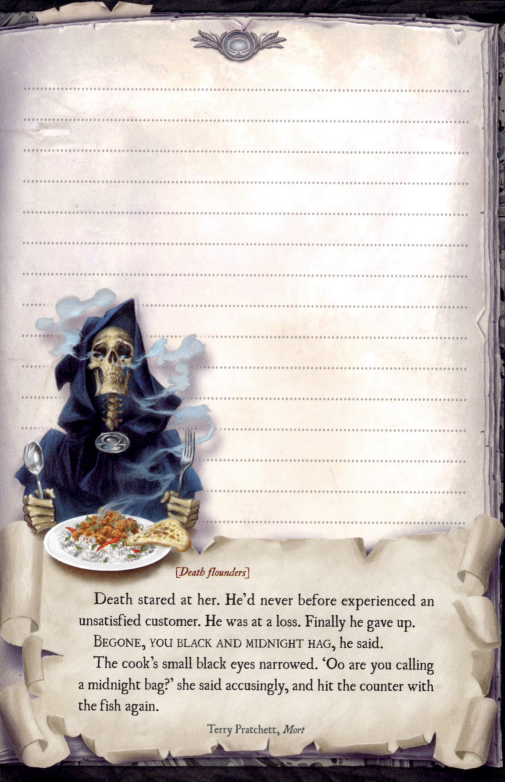

[*Death flounders*]

Death stared at her. He'd never before experienced an unsatisfied customer. He was at a loss. Finally he gave up.

BEGONE, YOU BLACK AND MIDNIGHT HAG, he said.

The cook's small black eyes narrowed. 'Oo are you calling a midnight bag?' she said accusingly, and hit the counter with the fish again.

Terry Pratchett, *Mort*

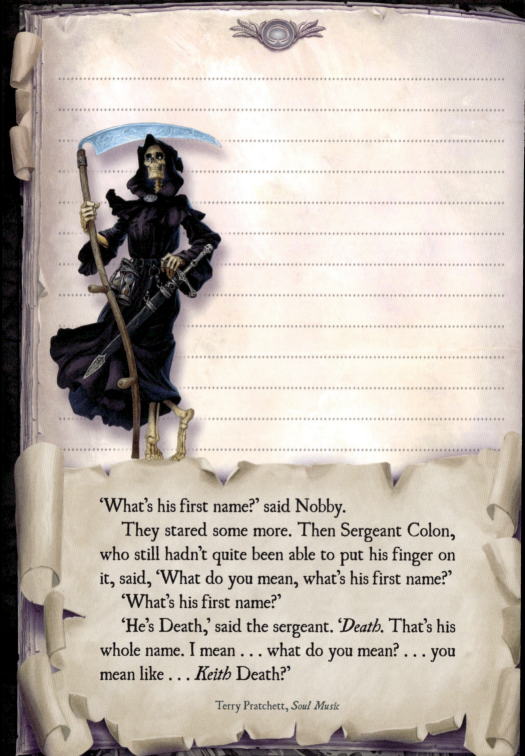

'What's his first name?' said Nobby.

They stared some more. Then Sergeant Colon, who still hadn't quite been able to put his finger on it, said, 'What do you mean, what's his first name?'

'What's his first name?'

'He's Death,' said the sergeant. '*Death*. That's his whole name. I mean . . . what do you mean? . . . you mean like . . . *Keith* Death?'

Terry Pratchett, *Soul Music*

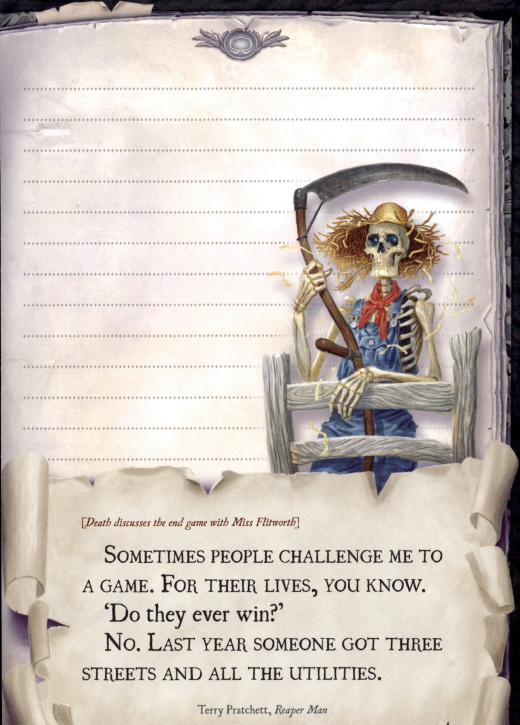

[Death discusses the end game with Miss Flitworth]

SOMETIMES PEOPLE CHALLENGE ME TO A GAME. FOR THEIR LIVES, YOU KNOW.

'Do they ever win?'

NO. LAST YEAR SOMEONE GOT THREE STREETS AND ALL THE UTILITIES.

Terry Pratchett, *Reaper Man*

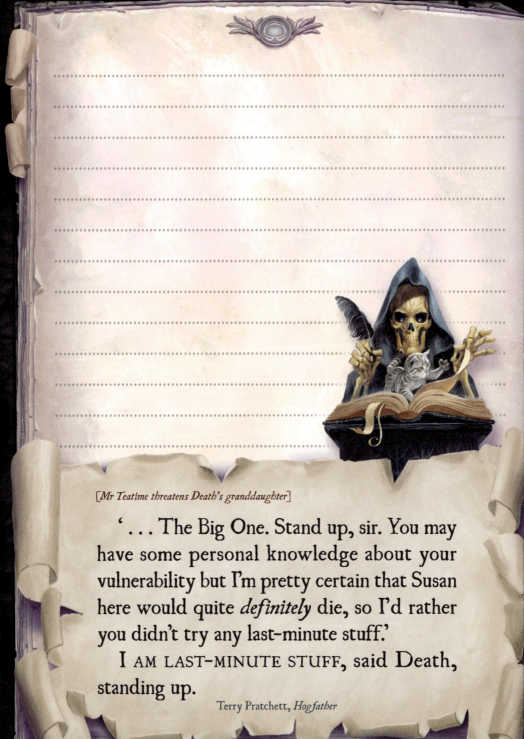

[Mr Teatime threatens Death's granddaughter]

'... The Big One. Stand up, sir. You may have some personal knowledge about your vulnerability but I'm pretty certain that Susan here would quite *definitely* die, so I'd rather you didn't try any last-minute stuff.'

I AM LAST-MINUTE STUFF, said Death, standing up.

Terry Pratchett, *Hogfather*

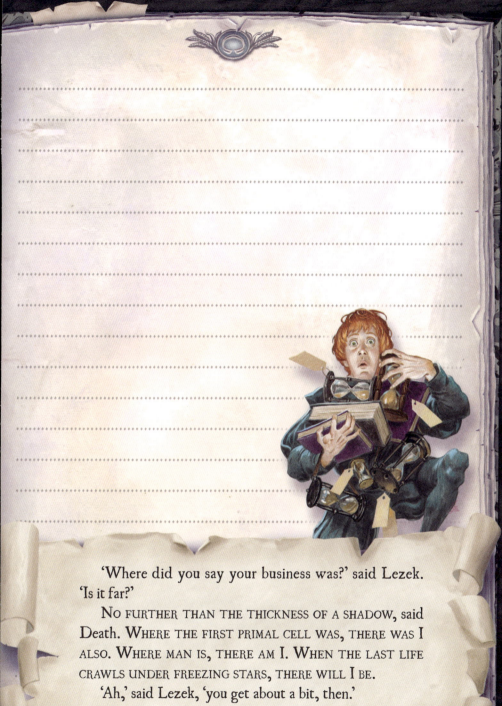

'Where did you say your business was?' said Lezek. 'Is it far?'

NO FURTHER THAN THE THICKNESS OF A SHADOW, said Death. WHERE THE FIRST PRIMAL CELL WAS, THERE WAS I ALSO. WHERE MAN IS, THERE AM I. WHEN THE LAST LIFE CRAWLS UNDER FREEZING STARS, THERE WILL I BE.

'Ah,' said Lezek, 'you get about a bit, then.'

Terry Pratchett, *Mort*

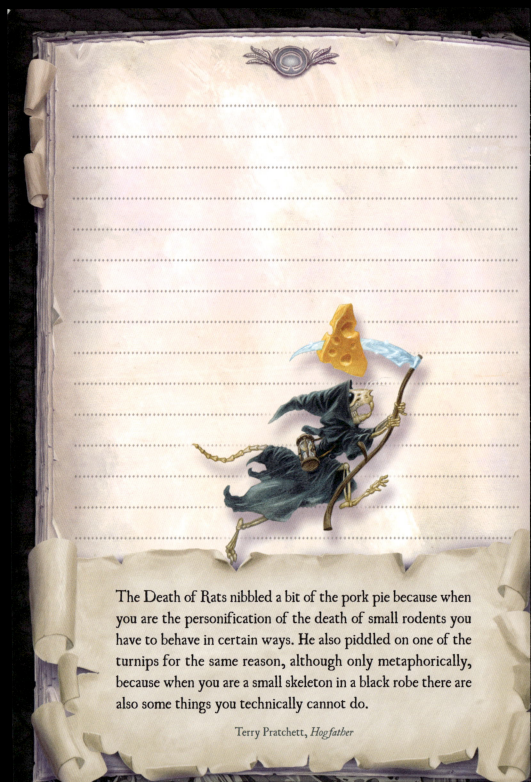

The Death of Rats nibbled a bit of the pork pie because when you are the personification of the death of small rodents you have to behave in certain ways. He also piddled on one of the turnips for the same reason, although only metaphorically, because when you are a small skeleton in a black robe there are also some things you technically cannot do.

Terry Pratchett, *Hogfather*

[*Isabell tells Mort how she came to dwell in Death's domain*]

'My parents were killed crossing the Great Nef years ago. There was a storm, I think. He found me and brought me here. I don't know why he did it.'

'Perhaps he felt sorry for you?'

'He never feels anything. I don't mean that nastily, you understand. It's just that he's got nothing to feel with, no whatd'youcallits, no glands. He probably *thought* sorry for me.'

Terry Pratchett, *Mort*

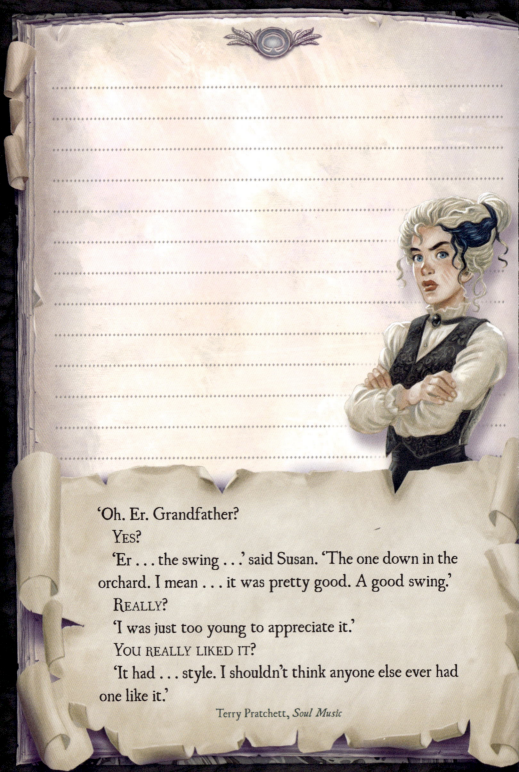

'Oh. Er. Grandfather?

YES?

'Er . . . the swing . . .' said Susan. 'The one down in the orchard. I mean . . . it was pretty good. A good swing.'

REALLY?

'I was just too young to appreciate it.'

YOU REALLY LIKED IT?

'It had . . . style. I shouldn't think anyone else ever had one like it.'

Terry Pratchett, *Soul Music*

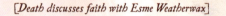
[Death discusses faith with Esme Weatherwax]

'I have faith.'

REALLY? IN WHAT PARTICULAR DEITY?

'Oh, none of *them*.'

THEN FAITH IN WHAT?

'Just faith, you know. In general.'

Death leaned forward. The candlelight raised new shadows on his skull.

COURAGE IS EASY BY CANDLELIGHT. YOUR FAITH, I SUSPECT, IS IN THE FLAME.

Death grinned.

Granny leaned forward, and blew out the candle. Then she folded her arms again and stared fiercely ahead of her.

After some length of time a voice said, ALL RIGHT, YOU'VE MADE YOUR POINT.

Terry Pratchett, *Maskerade*

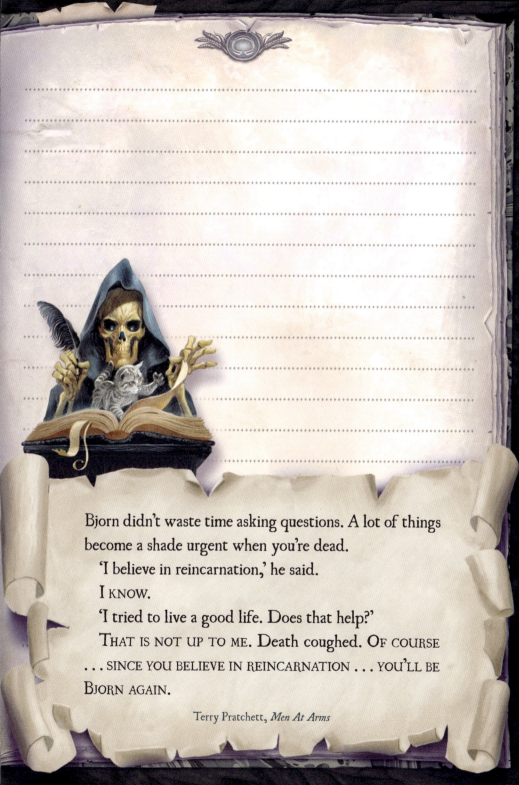

Bjorn didn't waste time asking questions. A lot of things become a shade urgent when you're dead.

'I believe in reincarnation,' he said.

I KNOW.

'I tried to live a good life. Does that help?'

THAT IS NOT UP TO ME. Death coughed. OF COURSE . . . SINCE YOU BELIEVE IN REINCARNATION . . . YOU'LL BE BJORN AGAIN.

Terry Pratchett, *Men At Arms*

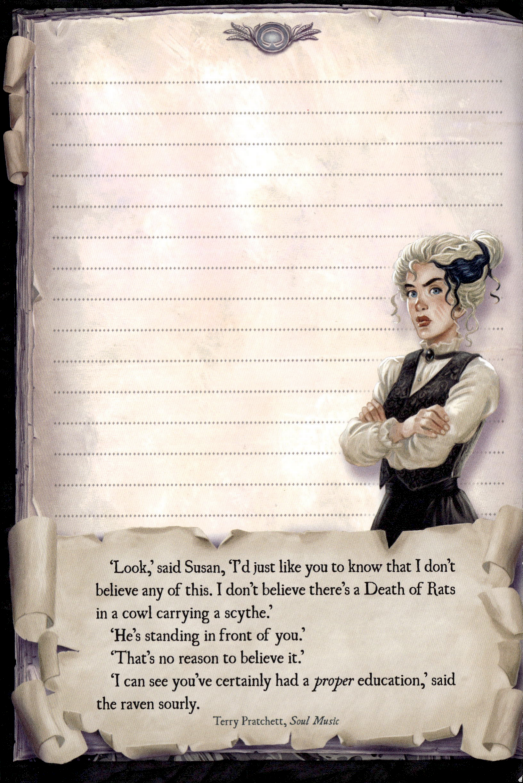

'Look,' said Susan, 'I'd just like you to know that I don't believe any of this. I don't believe there's a Death of Rats in a cowl carrying a scythe.'

'He's standing in front of you.'

'That's no reason to believe it.'

'I can see you've certainly had a *proper* education,' said the raven sourly.

Terry Pratchett, *Soul Music*

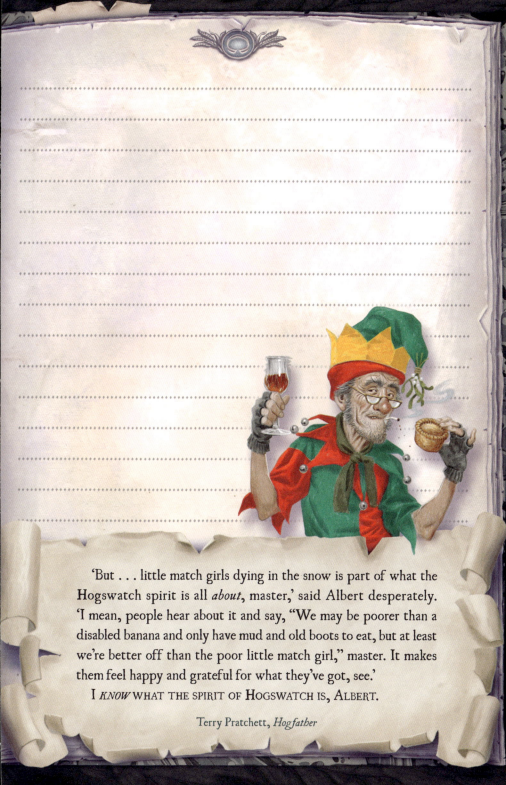

'But . . . little match girls dying in the snow is part of what the Hogswatch spirit is all *about*, master,' said Albert desperately. 'I mean, people hear about it and say, "We may be poorer than a disabled banana and only have mud and old boots to eat, but at least we're better off than the poor little match girl," master. It makes them feel happy and grateful for what they've got, see.'

I *KNOW* WHAT THE SPIRIT OF HOGSWATCH IS, ALBERT.

Terry Pratchett, *Hogfather*

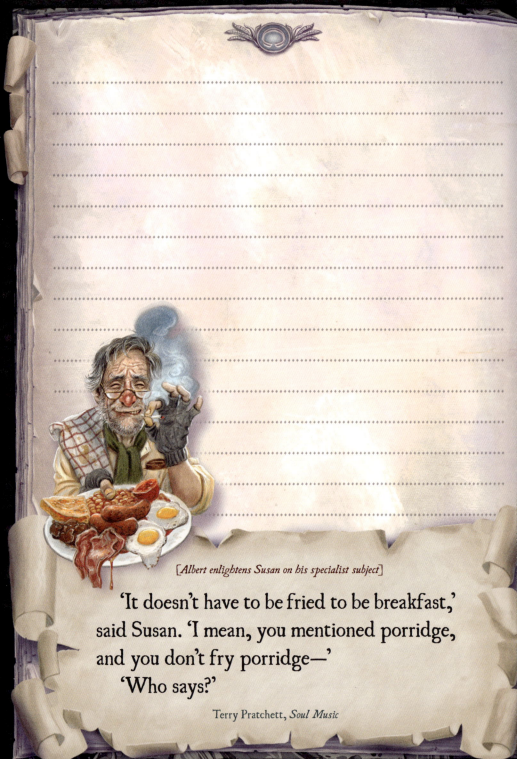

'It doesn't have to be fried to be breakfast,'
said Susan. 'I mean, you mentioned porridge,
and you don't fry porridge—'
'Who says?'

Terry Pratchett, *Soul Music*

G RANT ME JUST A LITTLE TIME? F OR THE PROPER
BALANCE OF THINGS. T O RETURN WHAT WAS GIVEN.
F OR THE SAKE OF PRISONERS AND THE FLIGHT OF BIRDS.

Death took a step backwards.

It was impossible to read expression in Azrael's features.

Death glanced sideways at the servants.

L ORD, WHAT CAN THE HARVEST HOPE FOR, IF NOT FOR
THE CARE OF THE REAPER MAN?

Terry Pratchett, *Reaper Man*

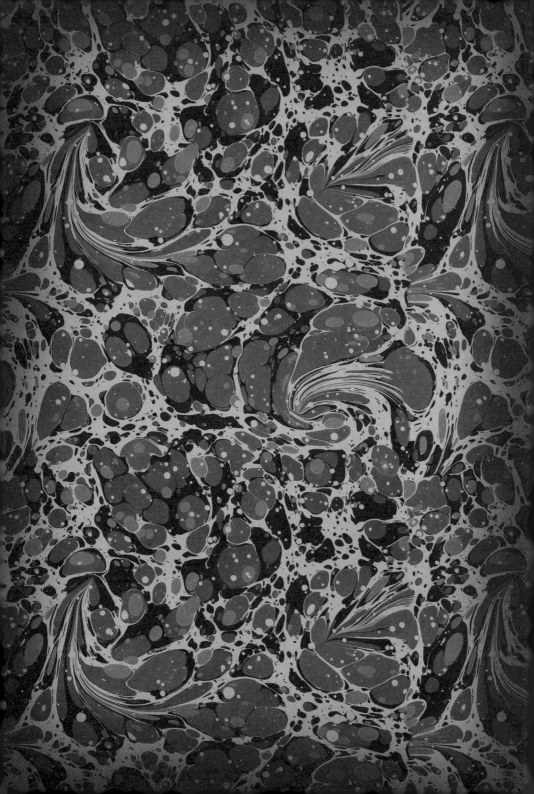